FOR VALENTIJN

Translation: Claudius Translations, Dave Cooper & Vincent Janssen Steenberg 2012

Copyright © 2012 by Lemniscaat, Rotterdam, The Netherlands
First published in The Netherlands under the title Valentijn en zijn viool
Text & illustration copyright © 2012 by Philip Hopman
English translation copyright © 2012 by Lemniscaat USA LLC • New York
All rights reserved.

First published in the United States and Canada in 2012 by Lemniscaat USA LLC • New York
Distributed in the United States by Lemniscaat USA LLC • New York

Library of Congress Cataloging-in-Publication Data is available.
ISBN 13: 978-1-935954-17-0 (Hardcover)
Printing and binding: Worzalla, Stevens Point, WI USA
First U.S. edition

Valentine and His Violin

PHILIP
HOPMAN

LEMNISCAAT

Valentine is taking violin lessons.

"Watch your third finger, Valentine," the teacher tells him.

"But otherwise you're doing very well!"

The town is celebrating the Queen's birthday.
Valentine solemnly takes the stand.
He plays **Ode to Joy.**

"**Horrible!**" yells a woman.

"**Hideous!**" shouts the butcher.

"**Get outta here!**" roars the mayor.

Valentine is surprised.

It went pretty well, didn't it?

Just on the outskirts of town there has been an accident.

The horse is old and feeble.

Gosh, thinks Valentine, the poor creature!

Maybe he'd like a little music …

He plays the **Allegretto.**

And guess what? The horse immediately jumps up!

"Thanks for playing your violin," says the farmer.

"I thought it was very ... er ... DIFFERENT."

Not far ahead, in the forest, there's a wolf.
He hasn't been able to poop for a week –
he ate too many piglets.

"Ooooohhhhh," he groans,

"I can't stand this bellyache any longer!"

Then Valentine arrives. He plays **Water Music.**
Now just take a look at all that poop!

"Thanks kid," says the wolf with relief.
"That was a R E F R E S H I N G piece of music!"

In the mountains Valentine spies a dragon ...
and a knight.
The knight is about to slay the dragon,
but then things turn a little ugly.

"Help!" he squeals.

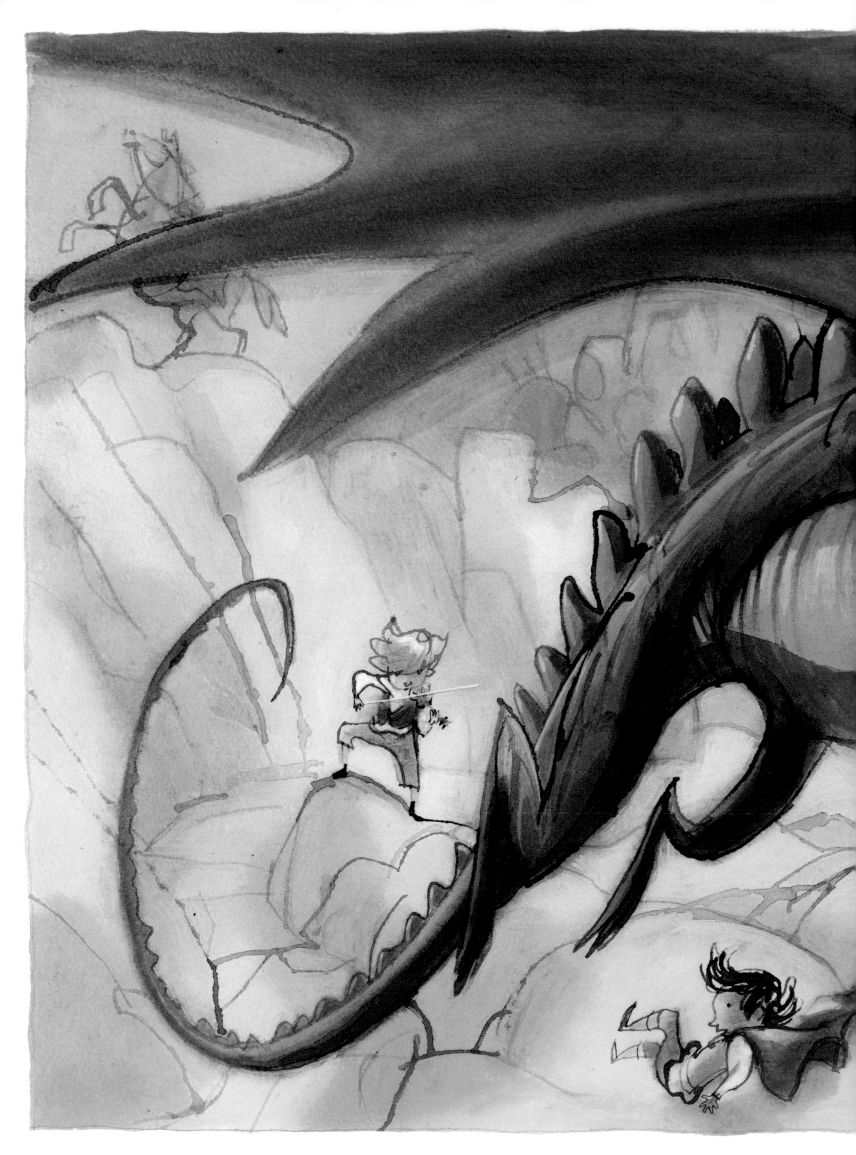

Valentine plays the **Waltz of the Flowers.**

The dragon takes off like a rocket!

"Thanks, buddy," cries the knight, **"what a cool piece!**

Want to come over to my castle? I have another job for you."

"You see, Valentine," explains the knight, "we're being besieged.
Wouldn't you like to play a bit more?"

That would be just fine with Valentine.
He takes his violin
and plays the **Marche Militaire**.

And the enemy retreats!

Valentine has saved the castle. Now he's a hero!
That evening he is asked to play for the King and Queen.
See ... thinks Valentine ... I'm pretty good!
I will give them the best performance ever.